Phineas and Ferb

Laughapalooza Joke Book

Written by Kitty Richards

Based on the series created by Dan Povenmire & Jeff "Swampy" Marsh

DISNEY PRESS
New York

Printed in the United States of America

First Edition

9 10

V475-2873-0 12160

Library of Congress Control Number on file.

ISBN 978-1-4231-2319-4

For more Disney Press fun, visit www.disneybooks.com
Visit DisneyChannel.com

INTRODUCTION

By Dave Barry

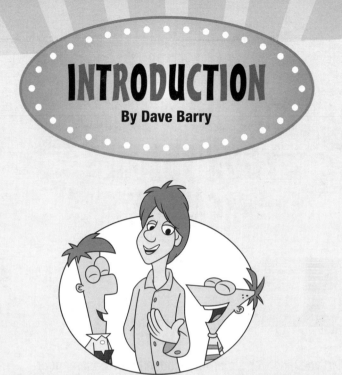

I know what we're gonna do today! We're gonna read this book of jokes. Of course, Candace will try to bust us. She is *always* trying to bust us. *"Mo-om!"* she'll say. "They're up to something!"

But before their mom sees anything, all the evidence will be gone. I don't know exactly what will happen, but I know *something* will. Phineas and Ferb will be part of it, and so will some evil plan by Dr. Doofenshmirtz. But luckily, as usual, it's Perry the Platypus (otherwise known as Agent P) to the rescue! It will all be crazy, but in some weird way it will all make sense, too. Meanwhile, you and I have a bunch of jokes to read. So let's turn the page and get started! But hey . . . where's Perry?

WHAT DID YOU DO DURING YOUR SUMMER VACATION?

Did you discover a mummy hidden in the basement of a movie theater? Build the world's largest roller coaster? Help your friend build a portal to Mars?

Didn't think so! Well, you know who did? Phineas and Ferb, that's who! These two stepbrothers certainly know how to keep themselves amused. (Even if it does drive their sister, Candace, crazy!)

And when they're not blasting off into outer space or surfing tidal waves in their backyard, there's one thing Phineas and Ferb *really* like to do—share a good joke. And this book is filled with them! So sit back, relax, and enjoy the laughs!

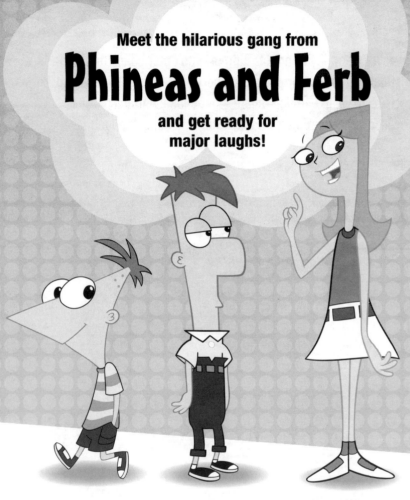

Meet the hilarious gang from

Phineas and Ferb

and get ready for major laughs!

Phineas Flynn:
Supercreative, he comes up with all the crazy ideas.

Ferb Fletcher:
Supersmart, he makes all of Phineas's insane plans a reality. He doesn't talk much.

Candace Flynn:
She is always trying to get her brothers into trouble. And she has a huge crush on Jeremy Johnson.

Perry the Platypus (aka Agent P):

The Flynn/Fletcher family pet.
He is also Agent P, and is called on
repeatedly to save the world from
the dangerous Dr. Doofenshmirtz.

Dr. Heinz Doofenshmirtz:

An evil doctor bent on
dominating the tri-state
area, but his plans usually
get foiled by Agent P.

Major Monogram:
The superior officer of the top secret organization that Perry the Platypus belongs to.

Isabella Garcia:
Friend and leader of the Fireside Girls, she has a huge crush on Phineas. But he has no idea!

Baljeet:
Phineas and Ferb's supersmart friend.

Buford Von Stom:
The big bad bully. Watch out!

The Fireside Girls:

This troop is always in the know and can always be counted on to accompany Phineas and Ferb on their adventures.

Django Brown:

Phineas and Ferb's hippie friend.

Jeremy Johnson:

Candace's supercute crush.

Suzie Johnson:

Jeremy's little sister. But don't be fooled by her adorable appearance. This toddler is trouble. Even Buford is scared of her!

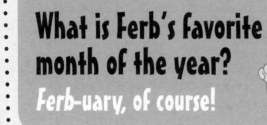

What is Ferb's favorite month of the year?
Ferb-uary, of course!

Phineas: **Knock-knock.**

Candace: **Who's there?**

Phineas: **Yodelay-hee**

Candace: **Yodelay-hee who?**

Phineas: **I didn't know you could yodel, Candace!**

Candace: **Knock-knock.**

Phineas: **Who's there?**

Candace: **Shirley**

Phineas: **Shirley who?**

Candace: **Shirley you're not trying to build the world's largest roller coaster in our backyard!**

Isabella: **Knock-knock.**

Phineas: **Who's there?**

Isabella: **Mike**

Phineas: **Mike who?**

Isabella: **Mike stomach hurts—that roller coaster was one crazy ride!**

Baljeet: **Knock-knock.**

Django: **Who's there?**

Baljeet: **Disguise.**

Django: **Disguise who?**

Baljeet: **Disguise crazy—he built a haunted house in his backyard!**

. . . .

Ferb: **Hey, Phineas, what's a ghost's favorite fruit?**

Phineas: **I don't know, Ferb. What kind?**

Ferb: **Boo-berries!**

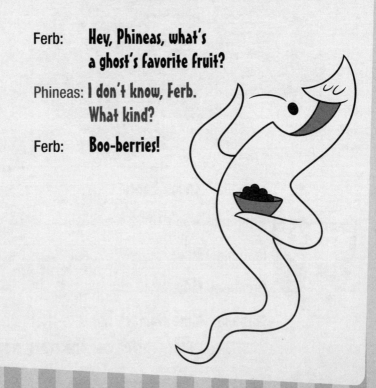

Jeremy: Hey Candace, why did the chocolate-chip cookie go to the doctor?

Candace: I don't know, Jeremy. Why?

Jeremy: He was feeling crummy!

Phineas, Ferb, and Candace have a pet platypus named

PERRY

To Phineas and Ferb, Perry is just your ordinary platypus. But little do they know that he also has a secret identity as Agent P—with underground headquarters and tons of supercool spy gear! His mission? To save the world (or at least the tri-state area) from the evil Dr. Doofenshmirtz!

Why did the platypus
cross the road?

To prove he wasn't a chicken!

**Which side of a platypus
has the most fur?**
The outside!

How do you stop a platypus from charging?

Take away his credit card!

What did Agent P say
when Dr. Doofenshmirtz built
a gigantic robot named Norm?

Nothing! Platypuses can't talk!

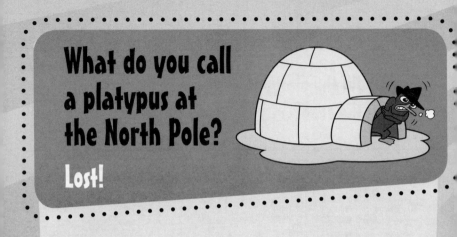

What do you call a platypus at the North Pole?

Lost!

What's the first thing that happens when a platypus falls into a lake?

It gets wet!

. . . .

What kinds of platypuses can jump higher than a house?

All kinds, houses can't jump!

When can twenty platypuses be under an umbrella and not get wet?

When it's sunny out!

Why did the platypus go over the mountain?

It couldn't go under it!

What is the first thing a platypus does in the morning?

It wakes up!

Perry's archnemesis is
Dr. Doofenshmirtz—

the most clueless evil scientist the tri-state area has ever seen. Just take a look at a few of his ridiculous plans: He attempted to dig a tunnel to China and set up a toll booth. (He just happened to forget about the Earth's molten center.) He tried to melt all the chocolate in the tri-state area. He tried to destroy all people dressed as sandwiches. You get the picture. And each and every time he is foiled by Agent P. But Dr. Doofenshmirtz never gives up. You have to respect him for that, don't you? (Okay, maybe not.)

What do you get when a mad scientist crosses a petunia with a great white shark?

I don't know, but I sure wouldn't want to smell it!

• • • • • • • • • • • • • •

What time is it when Dr. Doofenshmirtz submerges your home so he'll have lakefront property?

Time to get a new house!

• • • • • • • • • • • •

Dr. Doofenshmirtz:	Knock-knock.
Perry:	Who's there?
Dr. Doofenshmirtz:	Orange.
Perry:	Orange who?
Dr. Doofenshmirtz:	Orange you glad you're not evil like me?

What kind of dog do mad scientists like best?

Labs!

Dr. Doofenshmirtz's

outrageous plans make Phineas and Ferb's ideas seem positively normal! Remember the time Phineas and Ferb built a Perry Translator so they could understand what Perry was saying? They ended up with a backyard full of complaining animals who were finally able to say what was on their minds!

What's black and white and red all over?

An embarrassed zebra!

Why don't any of the animals in the jungle ever want to play cards?

There are too many cheetahs!

Why are elephants so wrinkled?

Have you ever tried to iron one?

21

How do porcupines play leapfrog?
Very carefully!

What's smarter than a talking dog?
A spelling bee!

What is a puppy's favorite swimming stroke?
The doggy paddle!

What's a bee's favorite candy?
Bumble gum!

Remember the time

Phineas and Ferb built a humongous haunted house to scare Isabella and cure her hiccups? There were ghosts, vampires, and even an awesome *Ferb*-enstein! It was spook-*tacularly* scary!

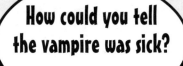

How could you tell the vampire was sick?

He was coffin!

Why didn't the skeleton cross the road?

He didn't have the guts!

Why don't vampires have any friends?

Because they are all pains in the neck!

What do you call a skeleton who won't get out of bed?

Lazybones!

Where does a werewolf sit?

Anywhere it wants to!

Why didn't the skeleton dance at the party?

There was no-*body* to dance with!

What has six legs and flies?

A witch taking her black cat out for a ride on her broom!

What kind of dog does Dracula have?

A bloodhound!

Why are ghosts bad at telling fibs?

You can see right through them!

What do you say when you meet a two-headed monster?

Hello, hello!

What is a vampire's favorite street to live on?

A dead-end!

Why are skeletons so calm?

Nothing gets under their skin!

Which monster is the best at dancing?

The boogeyman!

Why did the vampire stay up all night?

He was studying for his blood test!

What's the best way to call a vampire?

Long distance!

How did the skeleton know there was going to be a rainstorm?

He could feel it in his bones!

Or, how about the time

Phineas and Ferb discovered a mummy in the basement of the movie theater? (Never mind that it was just Candace wrapped in toilet paper. It turned out to be just as scary!)

Phineas: **Knock-knock.**

Dad: **Who's there?**

Phineas: **Howl.**

Dad: **Howl who?**

Phineas: **Howl we find the missing mummy?**

Why don't mummies go on vacation?

They are afraid they will relax and unwind!

Why couldn't the mummy answer the phone?

He was tied up!

Did you see how tense that mummy was? How could you tell?

He was totally wound up!

What is a mummy's favorite kind of music?

Wrap music!

What did the mummy say when it got angry with the skeleton?

I have a bone to pick with you!

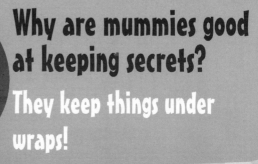

Why are mummies good at keeping secrets?

They keep things under wraps!

One day, Phineas and Ferb

decided to build a rocket ship so they could check out a star that their dad had named for them. The best part of space travel, according to Phineas? "The g-forces and eating dinner out of a tube!"

What's the most dangerous thing in outer space?

A shooting star!

What do you call crazy bugs on the moon?

Lunar-tics!

What are planets' favorite kinds of books to read?

Comet books!

Did you hear the joke about the spaceship?
It's out of this world!

Why didn't the moon finish his dinner?
He was full!

Did you hear the one about the rocket?
It got fired!

How cool was it when

Phineas, Ferb, and Candace traveled back to the time of the dinosaurs? Their time machine was destroyed, and then Candace was chased by an angry T. rex! Luckily, Isabella and the Fireside Girls were able to get them all home safe and sound!

What do you call anxious dinosaurs?

Nervous rex!

What do you call a one-eyed dinosaur?

I-don't-think-he-saur-us!

What do you call big meat-eating dinosaurs that get into car accidents?

Tyrannosaurus wrecks!

What makes more noise than a T. rex?
Two T. rexes!

Why did the triceratops need a bandage?
He had a dino-sore!

41

Surf's Up!

Phineas and Ferb once built an entire beach—complete with sand, palm trees, and waves for surfing—in the backyard. Even Candace had an amazing time!

Why wouldn't the shrimp share with the dolphin?

She was *shellfish!*

43

Why do fish swim in saltwater?
Because pepper makes them sneeze!

What do you call a shrimp with three eyes?
A shriiimp!

What do you call a witch who lives on the beach?

A sand-witch!

Hey, we're almost done!

But here are a few more jokes before we go!

Why is six afraid of seven?

Because seven ate nine!

Why are fish so smart?

Because they live in schools!

What kind of cheese is made backwards?

Edam!

Why did the banana have to go to the doctor's office?

It didn't peel well!